W9-AXX-919

TO:

FROM:

 Published in the United States
by Puppy Dogs & Ice Cream, Inc.
ISBN: 978-1-949474-57-2
Edition: August 2019

For all inquiries, please contact us at:
info@puppysmiles.org

The Super Tiny Ghost
OCTOBER
27
Illustrated by:
Catty Flores
Written by:
Marilee Joy Mayfield

Once there was a super tiny ghost
He booed and screamed and moaned the most,
But no one noticed he was there
Not even children paused to stare.

uuuuhhhh
SCHOOL

He tried with all his tiny might
To scare them in their beds at night,
But they just thought he was a sheet
With big, black eyes and hidden feet.

uuuuhhh
uuuuhhh

He made a list of things to try
To make the humans scream and cry,
But everything he tried to do
Backfired and made him feel blue.

56. Turn the Tv on and off...
57. Make it chilly indoors...
Furniture fly around
66 Make the Knobs turn... turn and turn... and turn
103 Make the doors squeak...

He watched the witches with their cats
And listened to the vampire bats.
He tried to learn their ghastly tricks
By watching monster horror flicks.

Spooky
Really Spooky
BEST HORROR TRICKS
MAGAZINE
BEST HORROR TRICKS
MAGAZINE

He wanted to be really spooky
But he came off strange and oddly kooky.
Being a ghost just isn't any fun
If you can't make people scream and run.

SUPERMARKET
CANDY
BOO-LOGNA PIZZA
BOO-LOGNA

He even went to scary school
To study being mean and cruel,
But when he tried to terrify
They paid no mind, which made him cry.

scary school
Ghostly
Goblin
Gruesome

It would soon be time for Halloween
And in his heart he had a dream,
He wanted to be wild and frightening
With boos like thunder and eyes like lightning.

OCTOBER
27

So he floated softly through the door
Of the local party costume store.
Everyone would scream and race away
When this new scary ghost came out to play!

COSTUMES
TRICK
TREAT

They had scary monsters and hairy beasts

Vampires, zombies, and voodoo priests

Creepy spiders and spell-casting witches

And mummies all wrapped up in stitches.

TRICK OR TREAT
Dressing Room

He picked the best costume off the last rack
And stuck it inside a trick-or-treat sack.
When he tried it on in the dressing room
He was the perfect picture of doom and gloom.

TRICK OR TREAT
Dressing Room
$
TRICK OR TREAT

He had blood on his forehead and a toothless grin
Warts on his neck and bright green skin,
He walked like a mummy with a lurching pace
Only a mother could love that face!

TRICK
or
TREAT

When he went back out into the store
People screamed and ran for the door.
Now he was ready to frighten and scare
No one would laugh now--they wouldn't dare!

EXIT
DISCOUNT.

A few days passed, it was Halloween night
The streets were lit by jack o'lantern light,
And the humans in costumes, both young and old
Wandered into the dark, crisp, autumn cold.

TRICK
OR

The tiny ghost had the best disguise
But much to his horror and great surprise
No one he met screamed or ran away
They just thought he was there to play.

TRICK OR TREAT
Hi Frankie
Hi Frankie

Except for one tiny baby--her eyes went wide,

She let out a piercing scream...and then she cried.

And suddenly the super tiny ghost felt so sad

Making this baby scream made him feel bad.

So he stopped for a moment and took off his head
And popped out with his tiny ghost-head instead.
Then the baby started laughing and he felt complete
She patted his round head and gave him a treat.

Visit → PDICBooks.com/tinyghost

Thank you for purchasing The Super Tiny Ghost, and welcome to the Puppy Dogs & Ice Cream family.

We're certain you're going to love the little gift we've prepared for you at the website above.